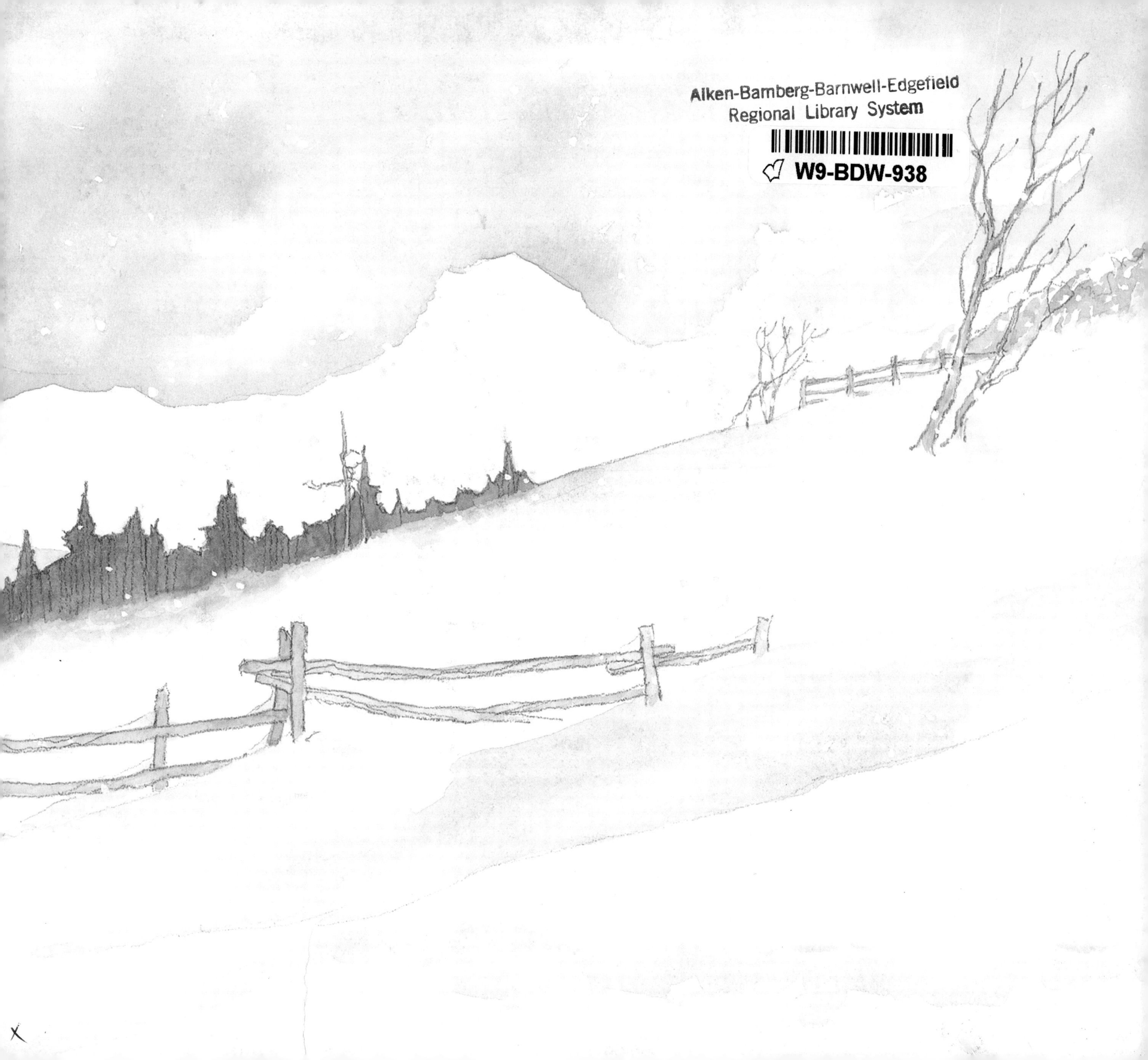

For Stephen and Kevin and Elias

With appreciation for the

work of Hope Ryden

≰ J . L .

———————

For Andrew
≰ B . F .

Text copyright © 1998 by Jonathan London
Illustrations copyright © 1998 by Barbara Firth

First U.S. edition 1998

Library of Congress Cataloging-in-Publication Data

London, Jonathan, date.
At the edge of the forest / written by Jonathan London;
illustrated by Barbara Firth.—1st U.S. ed.
p.   cm.
Summary: A boy and his father must decide how to protect the sheep
when coyotes make their home near the family's farm.
ISBN 0-7636-0014-8
[1. Coyotes—Fiction. 2. Farm life—Fiction. 3. Fathers and
sons—Fiction.]   I. Firth, Barbara, ill. II. Title.
PZ7.L8432At 1998
[E]—dc21   97-23034

2 4 6 8 10 9 7 5 3 1

Printed in Italy

This book was typeset in Veronan.
The pictures were done in watercolor.

Candlewick Press
2067 Massachusetts Avenue
Cambridge, Massachusetts 02140

AT THE
EDGE
OF THE
FOREST

Jonathan London

illustrated by
Barbara Firth

CANDLEWICK PRESS
CAMBRIDGE, MASSACHUSETTS

Winter came on a burst
of wind, and the snow
turned the world white.

That was the year the sheep
had to be scooped from snow
and bundled into the barn
to keep from freezing.

That was the year of the coyotes.

One blue day after a storm,
I woke to hear the sheep
baa-ing in the barn.
    On my way there, I saw tracks.
        Deep holes along the fence line.
        There were chores to be done
            but curiosity had caught me.

I snowshoed toward the edge of the forest,
   leaving our small farm behind.
I stopped to catch my breath.

And there ahead I saw it—and then I didn't.
Something fast and bushy and golden brown—
   then gone.
Coyote. I knew it.

Dad had said there were coyotes about.

"If they come too close they'll be dead.
   Coyotes kill sheep," he said.

I trudged on, searching
    for tracks in the deep snow.
The wind bit my face
    as I came upon a meadow.
And there below was Coyote.
He froze and I froze, too.
He lifted one paw
    and cocked his head,
    listening.

Suddenly he pounced
    on his own shadow and dived
    headfirst into the snow.
Only the black tip of his tail stuck out.
Then he popped up—
    as if grinning—with a mouse!

When he saw me he froze again,
    then took off like a streak
    of furred lightning.
My eyes burned with that
    glimpse of Coyote.
I was slow to turn back home.

Spring came
  and I saw no sign of him.
Then one day just before dawn
  the cries of the sheep awoke us.
We scrambled into clothes
  and out into the gray light.
Sheep scattered like
  huge balls of cotton.
  We found tufts of wool dyed
  blood red. Dad counted lambs
  and found one missing.
"Coyote," he said, and gazed out
  toward the dark forest.

When he got his shotgun
  I thought about what he'd said
  about coyotes coming too close.

We followed signs, drops
  of blood, fur on a thistle,
  prints in spring mud.
Dad was a great tracker.
But with his long strides
  it was hard to keep up.
My heart raced, but my legs
  raced even faster.

On Lindbergh's Hill we looked down,
   and there they were.
Coyote and another, nose to nose,
   some well-chewed meat
   on the ground between.
Dad raised his gun and took aim.

The coyotes licked muzzles
   and I blurted, "Look, Dad!
   The coyotes are kissing!"

Dad hesitated, but his finger held the trigger and began to squeeze.

I covered my ears.

Just then four pups
    tumbled out of scrub willow
    and swarmed their parents,
    wagging and yipping for life.
"It's a family, Dad!" I shouted.
    "Coyote brought them food!"

Dad didn't budge, but his eyes
were squeezed shut. Finally
he lowered his gun and looked at me.
"It's time we found a big shepherd dog
to run our fence," he said.
"We're a family, too."
And we headed for home.

That night,
  for the first time,
  we heard the coyotes sing.
And now, whenever we hear
  their eerie song,
  our dog howls back.
And sometimes
  I howl with him.